AF491205

Carl E. Miller's

Wanda, The White Jaguar of the Cannibal Jungle

The following story is dedicated to Spanish film director Jess Franco, Godfather of low-budget exploitation and B-movies. This book is loosely inspired by several cult films, including; 1968 (Gungala, the Black Panther Girl), 1968 (Samoa, Queen of the Jungle), 1975 (Ilsa, She-Wolf of the SS), 1976 (Wanda, The Wicked Warden), 1977 (Ilsa, The Tigress of Siberia), 1976 (Ilsa, Harem Keeper of the Oil Sheiks), 1978 (The Boys From Brazil), 1980 (Eaten Alive!), Jess Franco's 1977 (Love Camp), 1980 (Devil Hunter) 1981 (Oasis of the Zombies), and 1985 (Angel of Death).

February 7, 1985
Guyana Jungle

"Where is dad?" I asked in a very panicked voice. I was shaking in terror, I feared for the very worst- that he may be dead. My fear quickly became a reality, when me and my sister Sabrina discovered his lifeless, bloody body about one hundred yards away from the plane crash. The crash happened suddenly, without due warning. None of us saw it coming, and by the time my father must've noticed that there was a major malfunction, it was too late.

Sabrina was having a nervous breakdown, and I wasn't too far off from having one myself. I sat next to his body and cried for a long time, remembering the good times and becoming increasingly sad, knowing we wouldn't be having anymore. All he wanted to do was take us on a vacation to Curitiba, Brazil for Sabrina's birthday, and now I will never be able to speak to him again.

I was in the back of the plane, with Sabrina, furthest from the initial impact- but it was still a definite miracle to still be alive. The plane is now mangled and on fire, but the wreckage is only a mere speckle in this dense jungle. I glanced over at my Sabrina, who was really struggling to keep her emotions under control, understandably. But we need to focus on getting help, fast, before it gets too dark outside.

I have no clue where we are, but I still have my phone- which unfortunately has been rendered essentially useless due to no service and a nearly dead battery. "Hurry up and let's get moving." I said, as Sabrina was still crying. She gave a slight nod, but I could tell she wasn't in the right state of mind to travel very far, especially in this incredible heat, and very high humidity.

I didn't even know which way we should go, but after much consideration I chose a direction and we began to walk. Within minutes of walking through the heavy brush we were covered in sweat, and mosquitos began to land on us. I just wanted this awful day to come to an end, and get far away from this place- but the task seemed nearly impossible. There was no evidence of human life in sight: no vehicles, no fires or gunshots from hunters. The further we walked, the more we became convinced that we were completely alone out here.

Several hours quickly passed, still no evidence of human life in the general area. Now night is approaching, and with both of us hungry and tired, we decided to take a rest and continue our search for help in the morning. Falling asleep after what we went through was no easy task, especially considering we were in the middle of some jungle and feared being attacked by some wild animal at any moment. That never happened, but what did happen was even worse.

"Hey, just what the Hell do you think you're doing?!" I shouted, hoping that would propel the stranger away from my sister. When I was awakened in the middle of the night by very loud noise, I noticed some stranger was holding my sister down. The man had very little clothing on, and appeared to be from some sort of tribe.

His face was painted and he had a necklace on that appeared to be made out of teeth. The man said nothing, as he continued to grope my sister, and I looked for a large rock to grab. I spotted a rock large enough to do damage several feet away, and I made my run towards it. I grabbed the rock, but before I could even think about hitting the man with it, numerous other tribesmen appeared. Now the others were aiming blow darts at me, and then everything turned black......

They must've hit me with a dart, because when I regained my senses, I was in some kind of makeshift jungle house; inside a bamboo cage. Sabrina was across from me, but she wasn't caged. Her face was battered, her lip bloody, but she also had a very odd look in her eye. "Sabrina, what the fuck did they do to you?" I asked. But before she could reply, a very beautiful, yet eerily evil looking woman entered.

"Nothing." The woman said sharply, answering the question for my sister with a strong German accent. "Ve did nothing to her, ve simply gave her a choice. Ze same vhich you vill receive."

"What did they do to you?" I asked Sabrina again, hoping to get an actual reply from my sister.

The German woman looked at my sister and nodded her approval, signifying that it was okay for her to answer. "They didn't do anything to me that I didn't want." Sabrina said casually, then she smiled. Now I was more than concerned, I think these people brainwashed her.

"What is this choice you gave her?" I asked the German woman.

"Commandant!" The woman shouted, "vhen you address me, you must address me as Commandant."

"Okay, Commandant…. What choice did you give her?" I asked. She seemed to be pondering the explanation, a twisted grin plastered on her face.

"Ze chance to serve ze Third Reich. To stay in zis paradise that vhee created, and breed ze master race. Now your sister tells me that you are of German descent, that is very, very good. But being German is not enough, you must do your part in reproducing. You must be a good girl, like your sister." She said, giving Sabrina a little pinch on her cheek.

"I will do no such thing." I replied, while looking at Sabrina with a disapproving glare. I couldn't believe that my own sister would be willing to be serve as some kind of nazi whore, out here in the middle of this jungle. Whatever hypnosis they performed on her seems to be very, very powerful- but it will be a cold day in Hell before I allow that to be my fate.

The German woman was now growing very angry, completely dissatisfied with my response. "Okay." She said, pacing the floor in a very commanding manner. "If vuu will not cooperate, then I vill have you removed!"

She paused for a moment and studied my reaction, but I was content with what I said. The German woman stopped pacing and walked over to me, then she whacked her open hand on the back of my head.

"Vu know, I am ze Queen of zis jungle. Ze Jaguar, and to zis day, nobody has ever disobeyed an order. So…. Zis is an ORDER!" She shouted.

I remained totally silent, and this angered her so much that she began to make some kind of weird noises which seemed to more or less serve as a bat signal, because moments later several men were entering the room. Two of the men looked similar to who we encountered earlier, tribesmen. Only this time there was also a third man who had pure Germanic features. Both of the tribesmen had face paint, but this time it looked more like blood and one of them was carrying a human hand.

"Zis, is your last chance. Or next vill be your hand." The German woman promised, while the man showed me the hand, as if I didn't see it already. Then he began to slowly chew on it- seeming to really be savoring the flavor. Blood gushed out and the others all laughed, including the German woman and oddly enough Sabrina. I was blown away by my sister, this is unbelievably disgusting behavior.

I began to contemplate what to do, what to say. I mean I'm quite literally trapped, stuck. "Okay Commandant, I will....." I was attempting to make a fake commitment that I wouldn't hold up to, but now another German looking man barged into the room and interrupted.

"Commandant, I am ready." The man said. The "Commandant" glared over at Sabrina, and then Sabrina stood up and followed him out of the room, with one of the tribesmen following. The stare of the German woman

alone was enough to make my sister follow orders. Now the room was silent again, and then the Commandant began to speak with a renewed sense of confidence.
"So…. You vere saying?"

"Uhm-hmm-hmmm," my voice was cracking as I nodded, thinking of what to say. "Yes, Commandant. I will serve the Reich."

"Vonerdful!" She exclaimed joyously, "now I vill leave you to your task." The German man then stood up and walked towards the door, the Commandant now stared at me and I knew this was my cue- so I too walked quickly towards the exit. Behind me followed the other tribesman, and off we were.

The German man led me and the tribesman down a very overgrown path, on our left were several more jungle houses, and coming up on the right was some kind of water supply, and a possible showering area. I couldn't be quite sure yet, we were still too far away. But the closer we got, the more certain I was that it was indeed a showering area- because the German man was there, bathing Sabrina.

Sabrina was laughing and splashing around in the water, when she spotted us she gave a slight wave. I didn't return the gesture.

Suddenly the German man tugged at my arm. "This is it, go inside and sit down." I listened, and as I walked away I could hear him speaking to the tribesman, but I couldn't tell what he said. I opened the partial main door, then I walked inside and immediately sat down, as instructed. Within a minute the German man made his way inside alone, seeming to have dismissed the tribesman.

"I'm not here to hurt you, I'm here to help. I want to see to it that you escape. I'm no

Nazi!" The German man said before continuing, "I'm a Mossad agent. I'm here on a mission to bring Mengele down! My name is Efraim Friedman, but they think my name is Karl Shultz, a former SS soldier."

"Mengele. Mossad? I don't follow, I'm confused." I replied.

"Mengele, you know, the Angel of Death. The mad doctor who is largely responsible for the Holocaust. You never heard of him?" He asked and I shook my head.

"Well he's here, and he's extremely dangerous. He is performing experiments on women in these jungle houses. He's trying to breed a new master race, and create the Fourth Reich. The woman, the Commandant, her name is Wanda Kalacinski. She was believed to be hanged in 1946, by Polish officials, but they captured and mistakenly hung a low-level female guard instead, and she was more than willing to die in the name of the Reich, rather than give up her true identity."

I listened, but was very confused. "So what does that mean for us?" I asked.

"That means that we're in the presence of hardened criminals, very, very dangerous individuals. Not only are we amongst some of the highest ranked nazis, but they're being guarded by the Carib tribe, or as they're sometimes referred to; the Cannibal tribe."

"And how do you know all of this?" I asked.

"I told you, I'm with the Mossad. That's an intelligence agency based out of Israel. I've been on this mission for two years, living amongst these animals. I've seen things that you'd never hope for your worst enemy to see. This tribe that guards these nazis, they have no morals. Nothing is holy to them."

I listened again, but wasn't sure how to respond. "Well we have to get out of here, we just have to! But we have to rescue my sister too."

"Your sister?" He asked, "it's too late for her. She's one of them now."

"That ridiculous, I already lost my dad today, I won't lose her too." I said.

"Your sister likely already has the semen of the devil in her, I'm nearly certain of it. She is beyond brainwashed at this point. Now, she is totally convinced that she wants to be a slave to the Reich."

"She's confused." I replied.

"Oh, she's more than confused. Come with me, but stay very close, and very quiet. I will show you the house where she's staying. Then, before I help you escape, I will take you there to prove that your sister is no longer your sister."

I did like the man said, and followed very closely, and remained very silent. He grabbed two pairs of binoculars and led me to the back entrance of the jungle house that we were in. He opened the door and signaled for me to stay put, then he walked outside and made sure everything was clear.

"Okay." He said softly, then he waved me towards him. He lifted his binoculars to his eyes and began to look in the direction of the other jungle houses.

"Look, 10 o'clock." He whispered, urging me to use my binoculars.

"10 o'clock?" I asked. He sighed audibly.

"Look at the house that has three windows, do you see it?" I looked, I spotted a house with two windows, and another that had only one.

"I don't see…. Nevermind, okay I see it now."

"Okay, that house is where your sister is staying. Now I will help you make your escape tonight. I will get you out of here, that is a promise. But your sister, well… If you deem it absolutely necessary, then we will stop at the house she is in, and I will prove to you that she has changed. She will not want to leave."

"Well we have to try. What would happen to her if she stayed, she'd be killed, wouldn't she?" I asked.

"Yes, unfortunately if we can't convince her to go with you, then she will most likely be executed in the coming months." He replied sadly before continuing, "We have dozens of Mossad agents who are preparing to join me in the capture of Mengele. But this capture is very risky, and lives will be lost. It is very crucial that we wait until the exact correct time before we attempt Operation Mengele"

I knew we were in real trouble, and the moment that the tribesman started eating that hand all but confirmed it. When I saw that, I knew getting out alive would be a miracle, and I don't know how many more miracles I can depend on. After the plane crash, I should be dead. So should Sabrina.

Maybe I am dead, maybe this is some strange hallucination to help me cope with my own death. I can't be sure of anything now. If I'm not dead, and this is reality, then can I trust this so-called "Mossad agent"? Is he telling the truth? Or perhaps he is attempting to test my obedience to the Commandant.

These thoughts and many more were running amuck in my head, while I contemplated going to that house alone, capturing Sabrina and attempting an escape without the help of the Mossad agent. But ultimately, I thought better of it. There'd be no way I could guide myself through this jungle, I'm desperate.

 I chose to wait patiently next to the Mossad agent, and he would get up from time to time and peek through the window, or walk outside briefly. But when night came, and he still wasn't ready to help me escape, I began to worry.

"What are we waiting for?" I asked before adding, "I want to get the Hell out of here." He was standing up, looking out of the window and then he turned around to look at me. His facial expression was very serious, and seemed as if something was wrong. "Wanda is headed over to us right now, as we speak."

"What should we do?" I asked.

"Say nothing at all, let me do all of the talking." He replied. Seconds later the Commandant was barging through the door, along with two tribesmen who were guarding her. When she entered the house she appeared to be very angry, but her anger surprisingly didn't seem to be directed at me.

"Efraim!" She shouted, "ze Jew spy. Ze nerve to come into my jungle, how dare you." She looked at the tribesmen and nodded, then she pulled out a small pistol. She pointed the gun at Efraim, but he didn't seem fazed at all.

However that all changed when the two tribesmen began to tie him down and pulled out a knapsack to put over his head. Once his head was fully covered, the Commandant began to make her next move. She put her pistol away, then she turned and looked at me.

"Did you know that zis man is a Jewish spy?"

"No Commandant." I replied without any hesitation.
"You LIE!!!!!" She shouted. At this point she seemed so angry, that I thought she was going to kill me right on the spot. I began to cry and plead with her, but what's the point? This evil monster only cares about whatever sick, demented plan that these freaks have mustered up out here. That's it.

I knew I was fucked, hopefully not literally. But getting out alive at this point, with my only sense of help sitting five feet away from me on the floor with a knapsack covering his head, with two tribesmen standing over him while a female Nazi Commandant looks on, well the odds aren't in my favor.

The Commandant was now pacing back and forth again, walking with the nazis classic goose step. Then suddenly, without warning, she left the house, but I knew damn well that she would be returning very quickly. The tribesmen stayed behind to monitor us, and I was expecting Wanda would be returning back any second with a vengeance.

This unfortunately proved to be correct, but she wasn't alone. A man, who wore all white and appeared crazy enough to be in a madhouse accompanied her. He walked over to me and stared deeply into my eyes.

"You are German?" He asked.

"Yes, sir." I replied.

"Zen vhy do you plot against us, vith zis Jew?" He asked curiously, in a very soft tone. Which quite honestly surprised me, I was expecting to receive the same treatment from him as I did from the Commandant. But he has somewhat of a charm to him, he has charisma.

"No sir, I did no such thing. I would never conspire against you, or any of the German people." I said confidently.

"Ahhh." He said, "Zen you von't take issue vith killing zis Jew, zis RAT!" He shouted. Then he pulled out a syringe and removed the protective cap. I didn't reply, so he pressed the syringe to my neck, applying only a small amount of pressure. "Zis is gasoline, once I make ze injection, you vill be dead vithin seconds. Or... you vill inject ze Jew, and be a good girl like your sister. Your choice."

I didn't know what to say, what to do. How could I kill the only person in this jungle who wants to help me? How could I live with myself if I did that? I wondered about this, and I must've been pondering it for too long because the Commandant interrupted.

"Zis is not up for debate!" She proclaimed, pulling the knapsack off of Efraim's head in the process. Then she marched over to the man in white, grabbed the large syringe from him and placed it in my hand. She gripped my hand hard, never letting go as she pulled me towards Efraim.

"No, NO. STOPPPPP!!!" I bellowed as I kicked, screamed and begged for her to let me go, to no avail. I felt the syringe pierce his chest as the Commandant pressed her finger down onto mine, releasing the gasoline into Efraim's body. He immediately began to feel the effects of this death shot, as he started to squirm around and his face turned green.

Then, just like that he was dead. His eyes rolled back and his green face was left expressionless. He died a hero. He was trying to save my life, and I will honor him by telling the world- that is, if I ever make it out of here. That's a very big IF.

His now lifeless body made me feel increasingly sad, and incredibly sick. I started to vomit on the floor and that's when the Commandant grabbed my arm and led me outside. I wasn't sure where she was taking me, but the man in white, along with the two tribesmen guards were also

following behind. We didn't make it very far before she was making more demands.
"Go inside, now!" The Commandant said, as she walked me to the jungle house that Efraim said my sister was staying in. I did as she ordered me to and began to make my way inside, looking back several times in the process, thinking it could be a set-up. The Commandant thought that my fear was rather funny, and when she began to laugh very hard it set off a chain reaction- as the man in white and the tribesmen all started to laugh as well.

When I entered the house I instantly spotted Sabrina and became somewhat hopeful, but that feeling too would quickly pass...

I ran over to her and wrapped my arms around her, giving her a hard squeeze. "I'm so scared." I whispered in her right ear, trying to communicate my feelings before the others entered. "They're going to kill us, they already killed that man who I was with. He was going to help us. These people are monsters. They're Nazis, and cannibals." I continued.

"These people are not monsters, these people are our family." Sabrina exclaimed.

"Oh my God.. you've really gone completely mad, haven't you?" I asked, eyeing her curiously. "Look, we still might have some hope. Efraim said that there are dozens of Mossad agents who were planning on helping him, maybe if we can manage to just stay alive for a while, we can..." I was explaining, but was ultimately interrupted when the German man who initially took Sabrina away appeared. He arose from the dark shadows of the back room like some kind of Nazi vampire.

"MOSSAD!" He yelled with extreme anger, giving me a very hard shove out of his way. He rushed past me and made his way outside, then silence ensued. Silence in this cannibal jungle can't be a good sign I thought, as I stared fixedly at Sabrina.

"You shouldn't have made him mad." She said, shaking her head sadly before continuing. "It's too bad, because you would've been happy here."

"What are you talking about, you can't be serious." I said, as the front door swung open aggressively. The German man was back, and he looked mad as Hell. Behind him was Wanda, the Commandant, and they were also being accompanied by the German man in white. The two tribesmen appeared to have stayed outside to guard the entrance.

"Vhat is zis you say of ze Mossad?" The Commandant asked. I said nothing, I know that they aren't going to willingly allow me to leave this jungle, I'm basically a dead woman walking. So what's the point of playing along any further? That's it, I'm finished going along with this sick, demented shit. I'm done holding back my feelings. I'm going to say how I truly feel...

"You know what, you bunch of nasty, cannibal Nazi scum! I hope you all rot in Hell, right where you belong. You people disgust me!" I said, not holding back at all. But I kind of wish that I would've, because I don't remember too much after that.
They must've hit me with another one of those damn blow darts, because when I woke up I was completely naked and the German man in white was standing over me. I was in a totally different house, but Sabrina and the Commandant were both there also. Sabrina was now dressed like a jungle girl, and they were sitting down as if they were about to be entertained by some kind of performance.

I quickly realized that I was the entertainment, as the man in white pulled out an assortment of syringes, before choosing one and giving me an injection in my right arm. I started to feel very weird, almost as if I was drifting away into some kind of dream. Wait a minute, maybe it's a nightmare I thought as the man in white began to fidget with some kind of long surgical blade.

The man in white wasted no time as he began to poke and prod at me. "Hey, stop that." I said, or at least I think I said it. Did the words even leave my mouth? I didn't hear them. I did however hear giggles coming from my sister's direction. Holy shit, my sister…. For Christ's sake, she looks pregnant…. How long have I been asleep for? I wondered this very nervously, before being snapped out of my pondering by the sight of one of them filthy tribesmen. "Dear God, I ask you to please help me." I said, praying for a miracle.

A tribesman entered the house quickly, then several more followed. The room was now becoming full with Nazis and cannibals, and all of their sole focus seemed to be directed at me. Once the last tribesman entered the house he shut the door behind him and then Wanda, the Commandant began to speak.

"Oh Lord, Ve humbly ask you to accept ze sacrificial blood of zis pure German, and in return continue to grant us eternal life. And dear Lord ve vaited for zis holy day in November to also ask for you to bless zis new child. Zis, unborn angel who vill undoubtedly be ze future of ze Fourth Reich. Let this meal not only be plentiful, but also to heal us. Amen!"

"Amen." Sabrina and the man in white both said at once. The tribe people made inaudible sounds, but I assumed that they also approved of this evil prayer. Now there was no doubt at all about it, I was the main attraction. Everything was becoming very clear, I'm about to be the meal for these Nazi cannibals. They're going to eat my naked body until there's nothing left but the bones. Then they'll probably use my bones for jewelry.

I remember the first few bites, they felt so painful that I passed out. But before I lost consciousness, I recall looking down at my sister who was biting down on my big toe; a bloody-drool mixture fell onto the floor. The tribesmen we're also falling to the floor, licking the blood as it poured out. The floor had some kind of ancient markings, maybe runic letters. Wanda and the German man in white were loving every second of it, but

they weren't participating in the ritual.
Well, at least not while I was awake.

But then it seemed as if perhaps my own
prayer was answered, because I awoke to
the sound of helicopters hovering above that
sent all of them into a crazed frenzy. I knew
right away that these helicopters were not
friendly, and the panic on Wanda's bloody
face gave me hope. Wait, why is her face
bloody? Maybe she did take a damn bite out
of me, I couldn't be sure. I started to
examine my body, to see how bad these
bastards damaged me, then I began to cry
hysterically....

They got me. They got me real bad. All of my
toes have been eaten off, all of my fingers
too, and all the flesh is burned off my hands
and feet. I'm ruined, a God damned cripple.
"Oh no, please don't let this be real." I said,
But the pain was very, very real.

"Kill zem, kill zem! I command you!!" Wanda shouted, then she kicked one of the tribesmen and this seemed to work- essentially kicking them into fight mode. The German in white began to shuffle through a nearby cabinet and was handing each tribesman a rifle as they passed him on their way outside. I think he handed out eight rifles in total, and a battle was definitely about to be underway.

Wanda and the German man in white were terrified, not joining their cannibal guards through the front door, but instead opening a trapdoor that was in the middle of the floor, leading to a tunnel. They had their escape planned out, and when Sabrina tried to climb into the tunnel along with them, she was met with a swift smack from the

Commandant. Wanda pulled the trapdoor down behind her, then she vanished with the German man in white.

Gunshots echoed through the jungle, but I didn't have any hope left. Even if that is those Mossad agents, and they do save me- I'll still be a fingerless, toeless freak with third degree burns. Nothing could cheer me up, absolutely nothing at all. Sabrina was now looking through a window, she was debating what to do. She wouldn't even look at me, but I could see my blood still on her. That sick fucking pig, I hope they kill her! The gunshots continued to echo outside, and my pain was progressively getting worse. But after so long of hurting, my body began to go numb.

Even though I said nothing at all could cheer me up, that all changed when the trapdoor in the middle of the floor opened back up and the head of the Commandant appeared- but not her body. A shaky hand was holding her now, bloody decapitated head. The hand belonged to a man who climbed into the house with true confidence. He was dressed in all black, and following him was another man who was carrying the decapitated head of the German man in white. As soon as they reached the room they pulled out their pistols with their free hands.

Even being disfigured, dehydrated and starved, this brought a moment of great joy to me. "They chewed these girls all up!" One of the men said, as they both searched around the house- carrying the Nazi heads around with them like trophies.

"Are there anymore Nazis in the house, anyone in the backrooms?" The other asked. Sabrina looked at the man innocently.

"No, they're all outside." She proclaimed.

"Yes." I told the man, rebutting Sabrina's lie. "There are two more Nazis in this house." After the words left my mouth, everybody in the room was left in a state of shock, including myself. I couldn't believe what I was even about to say, but it had to be said. "My sister is a Nazi, they didn't chew her up. She chewed me up, along with the others. She's pregnant with one of them. So that makes two."

"What do you have to say for yourself?" One of them asked while pointing his gun at her. But she turned her back to them instead. She started to reach for something, but I couldn't be sure what.

"Stop!" The other shouted, "show us your hands." He demanded, but she wouldn't listen. Gunshots we're still echoing outside, however not as frequent as a few minutes prior. "Show us your hands!" He repeated. Then, left with no choice, one of them pulled the trigger and shot her in the back of the head. She died instantly, but this particular scene was so intense that I began to wake up from my sleep. Oh my God, I was asleep. I had a nightmare, that's all it was. Just a bad dream.

This turned out to be true, I was asleep. I must've imagined everything that just happened to me……. Because I'm still out here in the middle of this damn jungle, being slowly eaten alive by Nazi canni………………."

The End

Afterword

The character Wanda was derived from several different people, from both fiction and nonfiction. I blended elements from the fictional character Ilsa- from the 1975 film Ilsa, She-Wolf of the SS which was directed by Don Edmonds. However that character was based on a real life female

Nazi Ilse Koch. The film would spawn numerous sequels, and remains one of the largest influences on this story. The first sequel in the Ilsa series would come only a year later in 1976, with Ilsa, Harem Keeper of the Oil Sheiks. This film was also directed by Don Edmonds, and would be followed by another sequel in 1977.

This 1977 sequel directed by Jess Franco is titled Wanda, The Wicked Warden and is where I chose the name Wanda from. This is one of the reasons that I decided to dedicate this story to him, but not the only reason. Franco directed more than 150 films, and I would draw inspiration from numerous titles from his collection which I will cover below. His 1977 sequel would be followed by another, which would also be released in 1977 titled Ilsa, The Tigress of Siberia and was directed by Jean LaFleur.

After I chose the name Wanda, I wanted to create a title that had the same ring to it that those classic exploitation films from the 1960's and 1970's would have. So when I watched a rare jungle adventure film by Ruggero Deodato from 1968 titled Gungala, The Black Panther Girl, I knew I had to come up with something similar. There was something about the title that just jumped out at me. Along with the 1968 Samoa, Queen of the Jungle. So instantly the title Wanda, The White Jaguar of the Cannibal Jungle just came naturally.
 But the inspiration didn't stop there, so I would like to continue to give full credit...

Deodato would later direct Cannibal Holocaust in 1980, which is still widely considered the most controversial film ever made. This film did partially inspire this book with the cannibalism element, but really it was the other 1980 cannibal jungle film directed by Giallo legend Umberto Lenzi titled Eaten Alive! that I would borrow ideas from more heavily. In this film,.which focuses on the Jim Jones cult in Jonestown- is where I would get the idea for a cannibal tribe in the Guyana jungle which would essentially serve as bodyguards to this cult. But instead of being the Jonestown cult, I decided to add Nazis instead.

Now, going back to the main inspiration for this story, B-movie, Spanish sleaze director Jesus Franco, better known by fans around the world as Jess Franco, and his gorgeous wife Lina Romay. His 1977 film Love Camp had a plot that focused on a group of women who are brought by guerrillas to a prison camp in the jungle, where they are to serve the soldiers. The wardress of the prison is a female Nazi named, wait for it… Ilsa.

The sadistic, perverted Isla, is privately interested in some of the women, and interested in torturing the others.. When a guerrilla leader visits the camp, he falls in love with one of the "sex slaves" and decides to help her escape. But the wardress attempts to stop this by all means necessary. So the plot to this has some striking similarities, too many really for the main antagonist to bear the same name.

Franco's 1980 film Devil Hunter was about a Vietnam veteran who heads to an island inhabited by cannibals in order to save a kidnapped model not only from her kidnappers, but also from the cannibals.

Then the Nazi element would come from some true stories of high-ranking Nazis who fled to South America, including Josef Mengele, whom a fictional version exist in my story. This I credit to films such as the 1978 film The Boys From Brazil, directed by Franklin James Schaffner.

The Boys From Brazil saw Mengele, along with other Nazis, hiding in the jungles of Brazil and living rather nice. Devising a plan to create clones of Hitler. I wanted to go that route, but I thought Nazis breeding a new race in the jungle would be something new. Back to Jess Franco films, another title that inspired me to do a Nazi cannibal story, was due to his 1981 film (Oasis of the Zombies). The film was just a cheap B-movie, but it had hints of brilliance in it. Nazi zombies in the desert is basically the plot, and it works.

That leads me to the final Jess Franco Film that inspired this story, and definitely the most influential to this story from his material- and that is his 1985 film Angel of Death). In this film, he borrows very heavily from the aforementioned (Boys from Brazil)- where we see Mengele hiding in a jungle landscape, being guarded by crazed Nazis. But I wanted to also add a twist to that, so I chose to go with cannibal guards.

Thanks for reading!

I hope you enjoyed this story, if you did then please look up some of my other horror books such as; Eaten Alive 2, Motel on Murder Mountain, Fräulein Doktor vs. She-Wolf of the SS, Four Women for the Sex Killer and Frankenstein '30.

50